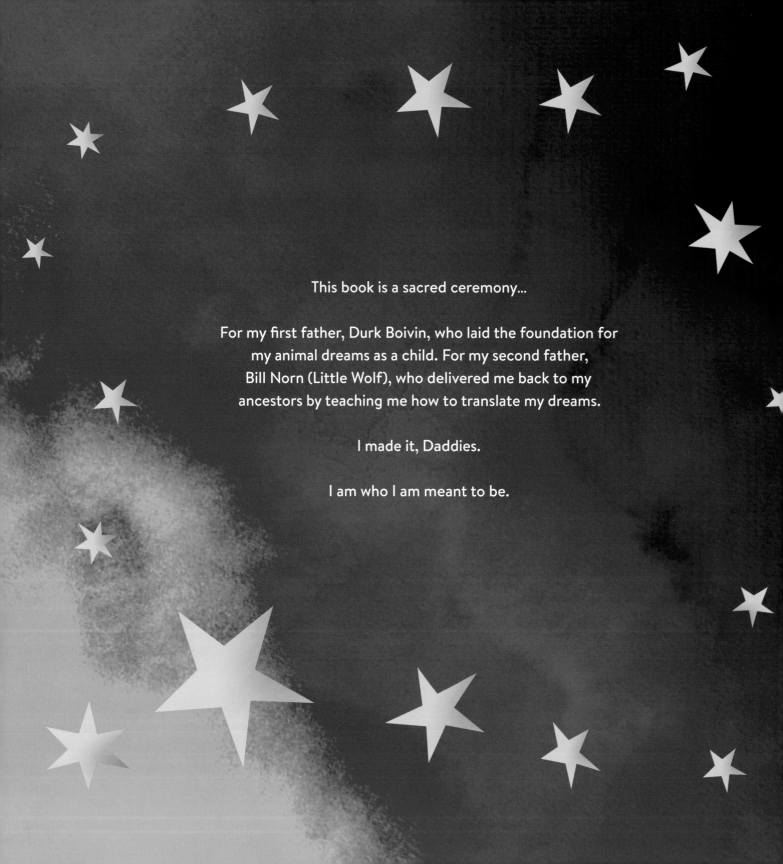

This book is a sacred ceremony...

For my first father, Durk Boivin, who laid the foundation for
my animal dreams as a child. For my second father,
Bill Norn (Little Wolf), who delivered me back to my
ancestors by teaching me how to translate my dreams.

I made it, Daddies.

I am who I am meant to be.

WE DREAM
MEDICINE
DREAMS

Written & Illustrated by

LISA BOIVIN

hw

HIGHWATER
PRESS

My first memory of you, Grampa, is of us napping in your hammock. I felt safe in your arms as we dreamed together. You taught me the importance of medicine dreams. "This is a gift that our people have always known," you told me. "There is medicine in our dreams. This medicine teaches us to be skillful in the world and teaches us how to face the challenges in our lives. These skills are learned from animals."

The first medicine dream I remember discussing with you was about Bear. Bear teaches us how to learn from our mothers. As Baby Bear grows older, he must leave his mother and learn how to be alone.

At first, Bear is scared, but his mother taught him well. He knows how to use his body. He can see far distances, hear the quietest of sounds, and run very fast. He can climb trees, and use his nimble paws to open many things.

He is also clever. He knows where it is safe to rest. He knows how to fish and hunt, and find tasty plants and berries.

Grampa, you told me that Baby Bear enjoys eating strawberries.
Strawberries are little hearts in the flora of the land. They remind
Bear that he is loved by his mother and loved by the land.

Soon he enjoys being alone and a delightful curiosity leads him through his world and helps him keep learning. He is cradled by the love of the land when he sleeps, and he is encouraged by the land as he learns how to live a good life.

Grampa, you said, "There will be times in your life when you are alone. Try not to be afraid. Remember your family has prepared you well. Even when we are not there, our love is always around you. All you have to do is look at the world to be reminded of our love. The world loves you as we love you, and wants to see you thrive. Enjoy your own company as you discover it."

I enjoyed learning
about the Hawk that I once
saw in a medicine dream. Hawk is
also a good teacher. Hawk teaches us
how to take a wider view. As Hawk circles
in the sky, she sees everything below her.
Because Hawk is given the gift of seeing
everything, she is open to receiving new gifts
in her life. She also remembers gifts
she has received in the past. Hawk
encourages us to open ourselves
up to new gifts that life will
provide, and remember the
gifts we have received.

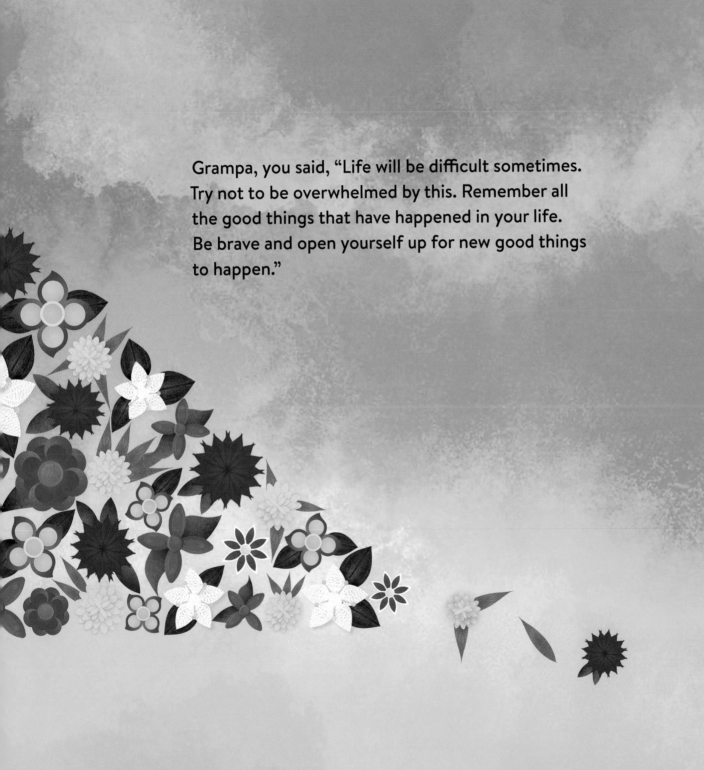

Grampa, you said, "Life will be difficult sometimes. Try not to be overwhelmed by this. Remember all the good things that have happened in your life. Be brave and open yourself up for new good things to happen."

You taught me that we share medicine dreams with Caribou. She teaches us about generosity. She gives her body to us for food, clothing, tools, and ceremony. She also teaches us to be respectful. We share the land with Caribou, so we must be respectful of her needs. We must do certain things to keep Caribou healthy. We must observe her quietly from a distance. We must give her space to roam, and we must keep the land clean for her. If we do not respect Caribou, she will not return.

You gave me good instructions, Grampa. You said, "Be generous with people. Be a good family member. When someone asks for help, use your body to help them. Use your ears to be a good listener. Use your arms and legs to carry things. Be respectful. Watch and learn quietly. Keep the land clean. Make your world a place where people will always want to return."

My favourite medicine dream teachings are about Wolf because you told me your mom called you Little Wolf when she was teaching you. Wolf teaches us to believe in ourselves and to live happily in a family. When we think of Wolf, we understand him as a fierce hunter. What we don't see is that when Wolf is learning to hunt, he fails more than he succeeds, but he believes in himself and keeps trying. He knows he must watch older members of his family to be successful. He knows he will learn from them as he grows into an adult.

Your words of encouragement are always with me, Grampa. I can hear you saying, "There will be times in your life when you will fail. Believe in yourself and continue to learn. Listen to your family even when you don't get along. When you disagree, be gentle with your words."

The lessons you taught me are even more important now that you are sick. Mom says you are in a deep sleep called a coma. You cannot talk to us. You cannot respond when we talk to you. And you need a machine called a ventilator to help you breathe.

The doctor told Mom that you will not wake up again. So, she and Gramma have decided that the doctor will remove the ventilator soon, and you will die.

I am upset. I don't understand why it is a problem for you to not wake up. You love sleeping, and I know you are enjoying your dreams.

Mom says I can go to the hospital to say goodbye before they remove your ventilator. I ask if I can take a nap with you one last time.

"Of course," she says, "I know Grampa would want that."

When I get to the hospital, I feel nervous. Everything is white and green. It has a funny smell, like strong dish soap. There are strange sounds: squeaky wheels, loud voices on an intercom, beeping, and adults whispering long words I haven't heard before.

When I get to your room, I am relieved to see you. You look like yourself enjoying a deep sleep. But you are resting in a bed with cold metal rails. The plastic tubes in your arms and the ventilator that covers half your face look strange.

I crawl into bed with you anyway. I close my eyes and dream a medicine dream for us.

The plastic tubes become flower vines growing out of your arms. The vines grow and grow until they fill the hospital room. They wrap around our hands, holding us together.

Your hospital bed becomes a canoe. The movement of the breath in your chest is the rocking of the river water beneath us. The river pulls us peacefully through a forest.

I am alone, and you are **gone** now. Like Bear, I am afraid, but I know you have taught me to **live** well. I like what you taught me about myself. I am a good **listener**, and I love to learn. I feel sad, but I know the world loves me as **you love** me, Grampa. I know you want me to be happy as I grow up.

I have been thinking about Hawk.
Grampa, you have given me many
gifts, and I must remember them.
I know there will be new
gifts. I must be open,
so I can receive
them.

Like Caribou, I want to share dreams with you, Grampa. I follow the instructions Caribou gives us. I am generous with my time, and I help others when they ask. I will always be respectful of the gifts the animals have given me, and the lessons you have taught me, so I know you will return to me.

I am struggling without you, Grampa. I find it difficult to understand the world around me. I know there will be times in life when I will fail. Like Wolf, I will keep trying. I will listen and learn from my family. I will speak carefully and with kindness. I will be humble as I learn from those who are older.

I follow all of your instructions, and finally, I find you in my dreams. Your body is different. You are now Little Wolf. You are happy to see me, and encourage me to learn and grow. You remind me to be happy in the world around me.

Canada Council   Conseil des arts
for the Arts   du Canada

We acknowledge the support of the Canada Council for the Arts. Nous remercions le Conseil des arts du Canada de son soutien.

HighWater Press gratefully acknowledges the financial support of the Province of Manitoba through the Department of Sport, Culture and Heritage and the Manitoba Book Publishing Tax Credit, and the Government of Canada through the Canada Book Fund (CBF), for our publishing activities.

HighWater Press is an imprint of Portage & Main Press.
Printed and bound in Canada by Friesens
Design by Jennifer Lum
Cover art by Lisa Boivin

Library and Archives Canada Cataloguing in Publication
Title: We dream medicine dreams / Lisa Boivin.
Names: Boivin, Lisa, 1970– author, illustrator.
Identifiers: Canadiana (print) 20200404784
Canadiana (ebook) 20200404806
ISBN 9781553799870 (hardcover)
ISBN 9781553799887 (EPUB) | ISBN 9781553799894 (PDF)

Subjects: LCGFT: Picture books.

Classification: LCC PS8603.O38 W4 2021 | DDC jC813/.6—dc23

24 23 22 21   1 2 3 4 5

HIGHWATER
PRESS

www.highwaterpress.com
Winnipeg, Manitoba
Treaty 1 Territory and homeland of the Métis Nation